Angela DiTerlizzi

Say What?

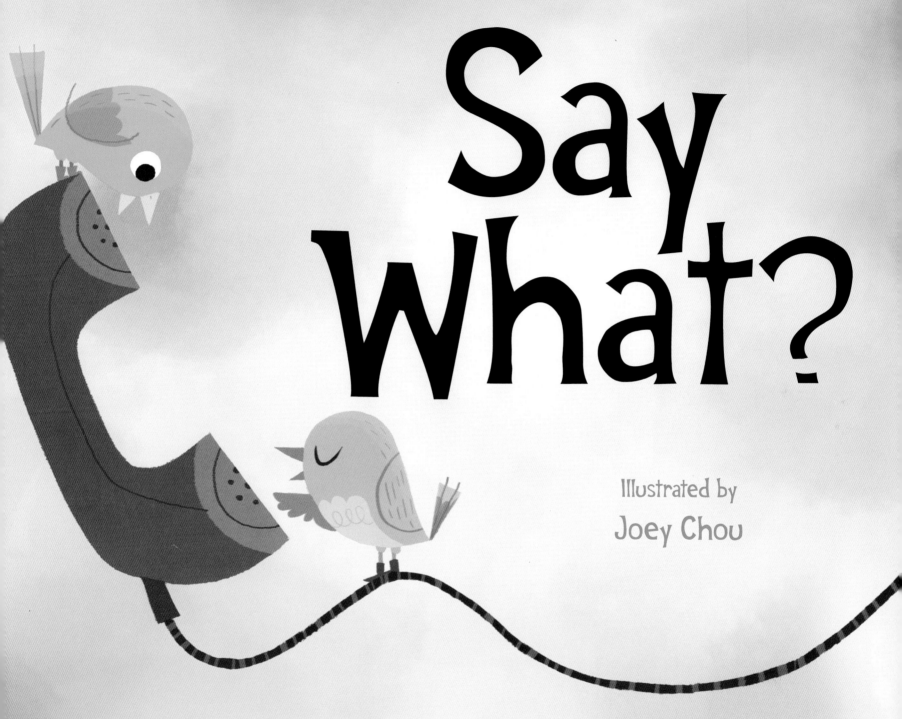

Illustrated by

Joey Chou

BEACH LANE BOOKS · New York London Toronto Sydney

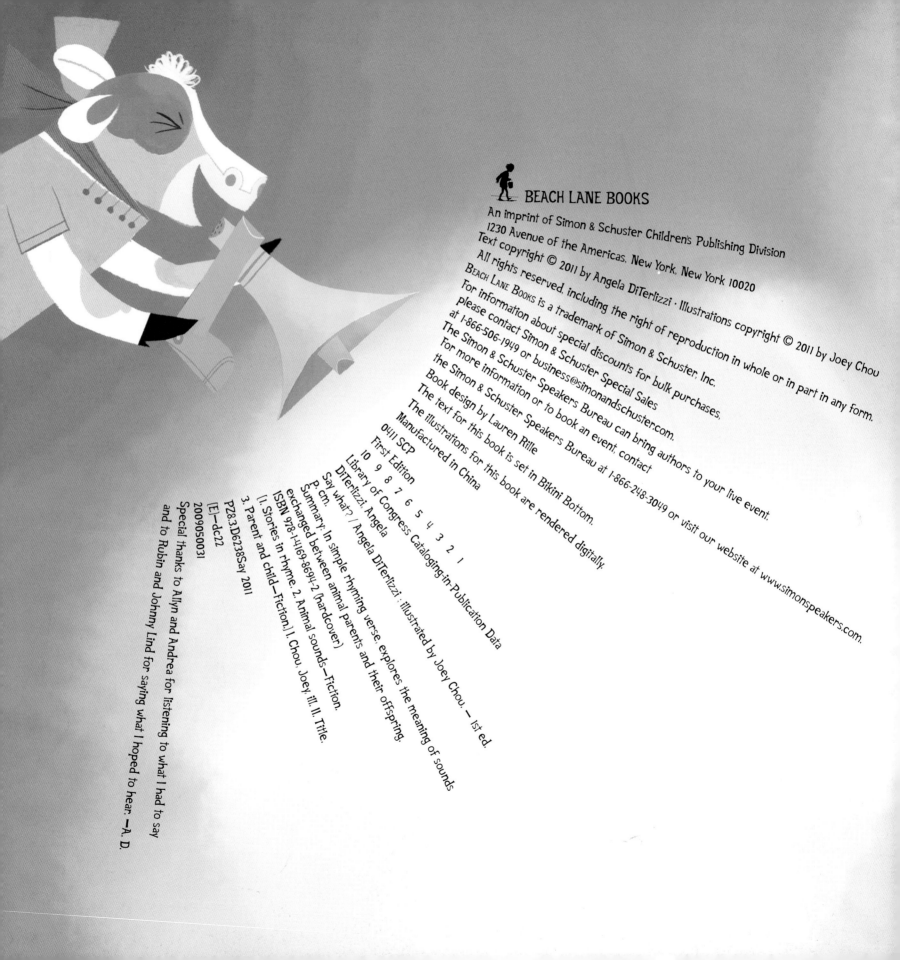

BEACH LANE BOOKS

An imprint of Simon & Schuster Children's Publishing Division
1230 Avenue of the Americas, New York, New York 10020
Text copyright © 2011 by Angela DiTerlizzi · Illustrations copyright © 2011 by Joey Chou

BEACH LANE BOOKS is a trademark of Simon & Schuster, Inc.
For information about special discounts for bulk purchases,
please contact Simon & Schuster Special Sales
at 1-866-506-1949 or business@simonandschuster.com.
The Simon & Schuster Speakers Bureau can bring authors to your live event.
For more information or to book an event, contact
the Simon & Schuster Speakers Bureau at 1-866-248-3049 or visit our website at www.simonspeakers.com.
Book design by Lauren Rille
The text for this book is set in Bikini Bottom.
The illustrations for this book are rendered digitally.
Manufactured in China
0411 SCP
First Edition
10 9 8 7 6 5 4 3 2 1
Library of Congress Cataloging-in-Publication Data
DiTerlizzi, Angela
Say what? / Angela DiTerlizzi ; illustrated by Joey Chou. — 1st ed.
p. cm.
Summary: In simple rhyming verse, explores the meaning of sounds
exchanged between animal parents and their offspring.
ISBN 978-1-4169-8694-2 (hardcover)
[1. Stories in rhyme. 2. Animal sounds—Fiction.
3. Parent and child—Fiction.] I. Chou, Joey, ill. II. Title.
PZ8.3.D6238Say 2011
[E]—dc22
2009050031

Special thanks to Allyn and Andrea for listening to what I had to say
and to Rubin and Johnny Lind for saying what I hoped to hear. —A. D.

For Tony and Sophia—
all I can say is I love you
—A. D.

For Julia
and all the beautiful things
you've said
—J. C.

How do we know
what animals say
when they say what they say
with their sounds every day?

When a cow says MOO,
does she really mean WHO?

When a lion says ROAR,
does he really mean MORE?

When a horse says NEIGH, does she really mean HAY?

They say what they say
in their own silly way,
when they say what they say
with their sounds every day.

When a sheep says BAA,
does he really mean MA?

When a cat says MEOW, does she really mean NOW?

When a duck says QUACK,
does he really mean SNACK?

They say what they say
in their own silly way,
when they say what they say
with their sounds every day.

When a bird says TWEET, does he really mean SWEET?

When a snake says HISS,
does she really mean KISS?

When an owl says HOO, does he really mean YOU?

What animals say, we don't really know.

But you know what I say?

I do love you so!